Glamour! Talent! Stardom! Fame and fortune could be one step away for the kids of Fame School! All the students at Rockley Park, a school for the pop culture performing arts, are talented, but they still have to work hard. They must keep up their grades, learn about the professional side of the music business, improve their talent, and get along with their classmates. Being a star—and a kid—isn't easy. Things don't always go as planned, but one thing's certain—this group of friends will do their best to sing, dance, and jam their way to the top!

Chloe's Big Success

The people around Danny erupted into frantic cheers. Danny was liked by everyone, and they were all thrilled to have a junior Rising Star. He was modest and hard-working and an amazing drummer. Chloe leaned over and gave him a big hug.

"Congrats!" she said. "It's fantastic! You're actually going to be on TV!"

Danny's usual expression was very serious but, just now, his face was set in an enormous grin and his eyes were shining. "Thanks!" he said. "I can't believe it ..."

Chloe was still congratulating Danny when all her friends started jumping up and down and cheering again. "I missed that name," she said to Lolly. "Who was it?" But, for the moment, Chloe's best friend was speechless and her eyes were wide with excitement. "Who *was* it?" demanded Chloe quickly, not wanting to miss any more of the names being called out.

In reply, Lolly threw her arms around Chloe and gave her the biggest hug of her life.

"Congratulations!" squealed Pop, joining in the hug.

"What?" asked Chloe, struggling to breathe.

"It's *you*!" cried Lolly, finding her voice at last. "You did it, Chloe. You won a place in the Rising Stars Concert!"

FAME SCHOOL

Solo Star

CINDY JEFFERIES

PUFFIN BOOKS

For my sister Ruth

with love and gratitude.

PUFFIN BOOKS
Published by the Penguin Group
Penguin Young Readers Group,
345 Hudson Street, New York, New York 10014, U.S.A.
Penguin Group (Canada), 90 Eglinton Avenue East, Suite 700, Toronto, Ontario,
Canada M4P 2Y3 (a division of Pearson Penguin Canada Inc.)
Penguin Books Ltd, 80 Strand, London WC2R 0RL, England
Penguin Ireland, 25 St Stephen's Green, Dublin 2, Ireland
(a division of Penguin Books Ltd)
Penguin Group (Australia), 250 Camberwell Road, Camberwell, Victoria 3124, Australia
(a division of Pearson Australia Group Pty Ltd)
Penguin Books India Pvt Ltd, 11 Community Centre, Panchsheel Park,
New Delhi - 110 017, India
Penguin Group (NZ), 67 Apollo Drive, Rosedale, North Shore 0632, New Zealand
(a division of Pearson New Zealand Ltd.)
Penguin Books (South Africa) (Pty) Ltd, 24 Sturdee Avenue, Rosebank,
Johannesburg 2196, South Africa

Registered Offices: Penguin Books Ltd, 80 Strand, London WC2R 0RL, England

First published in Great Britain by Usborne Publishing Ltd., 2005
Published by Puffin Books, a division of Penguin Young Readers Group, 2008

1 3 5 7 9 10 8 6 4 2

Library of Congress Cataloging-in-Publication Data

Jefferies, Cindy.
Solo star / by Cindy Jefferies.
p. cm.—(Fame school ; bk. 7)
Summary: Chloe is thrilled to be chosen to perform in the Rising Stars concert at
Rockley Park School for the Performing Arts, but as a solo singer she finds it challenging
to sing with a band, especially when her singing fails to impress her bandmates.

ISBN 978-0-14-241103-2 (alk. paper)
[1. Singers—Fiction. 2. Bands (Music)—Fiction. 3. Boarding
schools—Fiction. 4. Schools—Fiction. 5. Self-actualization
(Psychology)—Fiction.] I. Title.
PZ7.J3587Sol 2008
[Fic]—dc22
2007042303

Puffin Books ISBN 978-0-14-241103-2

Printed in the United States of America

1. An Important Day

No one wanted to be late for school today. But Chloe Tompkins was the first in her room to be dressed and ready. She couldn't wait for the day to begin, and she stood fidgeting by the doorway while her roommates collected their belongings.

"Come on!" she urged Tara Fitzgerald, who seemed to be taking forever to brush her hair. Tara raised her eyebrows but didn't reply.

"Finally!" Chloe sighed as she, Tara, and the Lowther twins clattered down the stairs and out of their dorm into the early-morning sunshine. They joined a stream of other girls all chattering noisily as they headed for breakfast.

"Hi, Danny!" yelled Chloe, catching sight of her friend as they arrived at the dining hall.

"We'll grab breakfast if you save us some seats," suggested Lolly, one of the famous Lowther twins and Chloe's very best friend.

"Okay," said Chloe, and she zipped across the room as quickly as she could, weaving her way through the throng of excited students. She joined Danny, Ed, and several other boys in their grade, and found enough chairs for everyone to squeeze around the table.

There was always a very lively atmosphere at Rockley Park School for the Performing Arts. The students were there to learn how to make it in the music business, so none of them were quiet and shy. But on this warm summer morning there was more of a buzz than usual, because it was almost the end of the school year and today was Rising Stars Day. After months of hard work, the students would hear which of them had earned the right to perform in the all-important Rising Stars Concert at the end of the semester. For some, today was going to be the best day of the year.

"Chocolate croissants," announced Pop, dumping a tray on the table. "Even the catering staff have decided today is special."

"I know I haven't got enough Rising Stars points," said Ed, "but oh well. There'll be other years." He reached out and took a croissant. "And one of these will *almost* make up for not performing at the concert."

"Oh, come on," said Pop, the other Lowther twin. "We've all dreamed of taking part."

"It would be so cool to perform live at the television studio," said Chloe. "And it could be the making of our careers."

"Rob is *bound* to get a place," said Pop. "He's *so* talented and *so* good-looking!"

"Give it a rest, Pop," complained Tara. "You're biased. We all know how much you like him."

"I do not!" protested Pop, but she didn't sound very convincing. She'd been teased before about the gifted singer in tenth grade, but she wasn't the only one who had singled him out. Most students would agree that Rob Copeland had a very good chance of winning a place this year. His voice had broken early and had settled into the wonderful, rich tones that all the girls loved.

"I still think *you* have a chance," Lolly told Chloe.

Chloe smiled at her best friend. "I wish!" she said. "But I got off to a slow start at the beginning of the year. Remember when I couldn't find my voice at all?"

"You've done wonderfully ever since," Lolly reminded her. "So you never know. You've got more Rising Stars points than Pop and me, and you're definitely Mr. Player's star student."

Chloe blushed.

"You *are*," agreed Pop. "You work so hard at getting things right. You never give up, and your voice is mega!"

"Still, it's usually the older students that win places, isn't it?" said Ed. "After all, they have more experience and are mostly better than us."

"You're right," agreed Chloe, trying not to let the twins' comments go to her head. But she couldn't help hoping that her last performance had earned her enough points to give her at least a chance.

The system was simple. Every student was able to earn points from their teachers for general good work during the year. Outstanding performances were awarded points as well. Chloe had been very pleased with her last performance, which had been at a big outdoor charity event to raise money for an African school. It was what she loved most of all, to be out there alone onstage, totally independent of any other performers. *Could* she have done well enough to overtake some seriously good older students? She had to admit that it was unlikely.

"I think the only one of us who might have earned a place is Danny," she said, smiling at the most talented drummer in their grade.

"Well, we'll find out soon," said Danny's friend Marmalade. "It's almost time." He got to his feet and reached for his crutches. Chloe felt a stab of sympathy for Marmalade. He was an awesome dancer and had had a good chance of winning a place himself, but he had been injured while fooling around one day, and was now out of the running. You didn't just need to keep focused and work hard in this business, it was vital to stay fit and healthy, too.

"Let's go," said Lolly. "I can't bear the suspense. And if we go now, we should get good seats."

They made their way to the theater at Marmalade's pace and sat down together. They were only just in time. Lots of other students had decided to arrive early for assembly today as well.

The first few minutes were taken up with the usual announcements and school business. Pop looked at Chloe and rolled her eyes. She didn't have a lot of patience at the best of times, and today was certainly no exception.

Once Mrs. Sharkey, the principal, had finished dealing with the announcements, she paused. She didn't need to wait to get everyone's attention because every student knew that the Rising Stars announcement would be next. The small theater was so quiet, it could have been empty. Everyone was silently urging the principal to go ahead and make the announcement, but Mrs. Sharkey knew how to work an audience as well as anyone, and she raised the tension by making them wait.

"And now," she said eventually into the electric silence. "The Rising Stars Concert."

Chloe put her hands over her mouth to stop herself from letting out a squeak of excitement.

"It has been very close this year," said Mrs. Sharkey. "And more students than usual were in the running. But after adding up all the points won for progress throughout the year and for excellence in performance, we have these names." She paused again. Chloe could hardly bear it.

"Rob Copeland."

Pop let out a yelp and began clapping wildly, as did the rest of the school. Chloe and Lolly exchanged amused glances. Pop would be on a high for the rest of the day with that news to keep her happy.

Mrs. Sharkey waited for the applause to die away before she read out the next name. "Isla Duncan."

Isla was in her last year at Rockley Park and was a

great singer. Chloe felt really happy for her and applauded along with everyone else.

"Danny James."

Chloe let out a huge squeal. "Danny! You've been chosen!"

The people around Danny erupted into frantic cheers. Danny was liked by everyone, and they were all thrilled to have a junior Rising Star. He was modest and hardworking and an amazing drummer. Chloe leaned over and gave him a big hug.

"Congrats!" she said. "It's fantastic! You're actually going to be on TV!"

Danny's usual expression was very serious, but, just now, his face was set in an enormous grin and his eyes were shining. "Thanks!" he said. "I can't believe it ..."

Chloe was still congratulating Danny when all her friends started jumping up and down and cheering again. "I missed that name," she said to Lolly. "Who was it?" But, for the moment, Chloe's best friend was speechless and her eyes were wide with excitement.

"Who *was* it?" demanded Chloe quickly, not wanting to miss any more of the names being called out.

In reply, Lolly threw her arms around Chloe and gave her the biggest hug of her life.

"Congratulations!" squealed Pop, joining in the hug.

"What?" asked Chloe, struggling to breathe.

"It's *you*!" cried Lolly, finding her voice at last. "You did it, Chloe. You won a place in the Rising Stars Concert!"

2. A New Rising Star

"That's so amazing!" said Lolly. "You're such a star. I knew you had a chance."

Chloe could feel her heart pounding under her T-shirt. Was it true? Had she *really* gotten enough Rising Stars points?

"Well," said Danny, still grinning widely. "How cool is that? Both of us Rising Stars at the end of our first year at Rockley Park! No wonder we both got scholarships."

Chloe tried to look shocked. "Danny!" she said. But he wasn't being bigheaded. Danny was being honest, as he always was. Everyone knew that scholarships weren't handed out to simply anyone. Danny and

Chloe's talents had been recognized before they came to the school and now, with all their hard work, they were fulfilling the teachers' faith in them.

Even so, Chloe did feel incredibly lucky to have become a Rising Star in her first year. It would be exciting enough if it were just a matter of recording a television program, but more exciting than that was the invited studio audience. Alongside other people from the music industry, there would be A&R people— special recording-company scouts. A&R stood for Artists and Repertoire. It was their job to spot any likely talent, and as a result, some Rising Stars in the past had been offered recording contracts on the spot.

"Sssh! Sssh."

Mrs. Sharkey was speaking again, and slowly everyone calmed down and fell silent. "To round off our assembly, there will now be a short performance from two of our dancers," she said. "And right afterward there will be a meeting for this year's Rising Stars. Everyone whose name I've called out should stay behind so that Mr. Player and Judge Jim Henson can discuss the details of the concert. That's all. Everyone else can make their way quietly to their first class as soon as the performance is over."

Chloe couldn't concentrate on the dance. All she could think about was the fact that she was going to be in the Rising Stars Concert. She could hardly believe it. A year ago, she had been at an ordinary school with little chance of making it as a singer. Now she was at Rockley Park, the best school in the world, and she was living her dream of becoming a star.

The rest of the assembly passed in a daze for Chloe, but eventually it was over and the majority of the students started to file out.

"Good luck!" said Lolly, pausing to hug Chloe again before disappearing off to class with Pop.

Chloe and Danny exchanged excited grins. Almost everyone had gone now. Chloe counted up how many students had been chosen as Rising Stars. There were sixteen, all of them older than her and Danny. Several were in their last year at school. They were practically grown up.

"Come and gather around," called Mr. Player. The singing teacher was standing down by the front row of seats along with Judge Jim, the Head of the Rock Department. All the Rising Stars made their way quickly to the front.

"This is just a brief meetin' to get you all together," said Judge Jim, smiling at them all. "First thing is, congratulations! Every one of you has earned your place here with lots of hard work, and I know you'll be prepared to work even harder at makin' this showcase of Rockley Park's talent the best it can be."

Chloe listened carefully to everything Judge Jim said. She was very conscious of being one of the youngest there and didn't want to be the one act to let the whole concert down.

"Now, as you probably know," said Judge Jim, "the TV program is only thirty minutes long, and they like to intersperse some general shots of the performers between each act, which cuts down the performance time even more. So we have to work out how to give all sixteen of you the best chance to show your individual performance skills in such a short time."

"There will be time for just six acts, so the only way we can include you all is to have you share your performances," said Mr. Player.

Several of the older students nodded understandingly, but Chloe found that her mouth was suddenly dry with apprehension.

"Judge Jim and I already have some thoughts, so let's get you into groups and discuss how best to assemble you into acts," said Mr. Player. "Singers, come over here. Musicians, could you wait over there?"

Danny seemed quite happy to be with musicians much older than him. Nothing much bothered him as long as he could play his beloved drums. He was used to performing with other people, but Chloe didn't feel anywhere near as confident. She was very anxious as she joined the rest of the singers.

Suddenly, being a Rising Star didn't feel quite as wonderful as she'd thought it would. It hadn't occurred to Chloe that she might have to sing with other people. She had assumed that being chosen would mean performing in the way you did best, which for Chloe was singing solo with a backing track.

How can I possibly perform with these students? thought Chloe. *They're all so grown up.*

She was sure her talent would never stand out next to them. *It's not fair!* she thought to herself miserably. *The A&R people won't notice me at all. I didn't realize being a Rising Star was going to be like this!*

Mr. Player glanced toward Chloe and then away again. That made her even more nervous. Was he going to tell her that they'd made a mistake and that she wasn't going to be a Rising Star after all? She began to think it would almost be a relief if he did. But she soon changed her mind. Everyone wanted the chance of being a Rising Star, and now that she had gotten it, Chloe was determined to hang on and hope that it turned out well.

"Right," said Judge Jim. "We don't want to keep you too long. We can fine-tune this later, but we wanted to try to give you some idea of how we propose to squeeze sixteen of you into six acts."

He grinned at the musicians. "I realize that each of you has your own particular style," he said. "And we'll do our best to let you show off your individuality at the concert, but everyone is goin' to have to compromise a little. Luckily, we have two drummers and I think we can make two quite different bands out of you. I know what I think would work well, but why don't you discuss it among yourselves and see if you can come up with a solution you're all happy with?"

"Yes, please," agreed one of the senior boys, who Chloe knew played guitar. He looked at his fellow musicians and they all nodded.

"Okay. Good."

Next, Judge Jim turned to the singers. "You're more of a problem," he said, "because Mr. Player tells me you are all soloists."

"I'm happy to sing with Rob," one of the girls volunteered right away.

"Sounds good to me," Rob agreed.

Mr. Player looked pleased.

"Thank you," said Judge Jim.

"If one of the bands needs a vocalist, I'd love to do that," said the other boy.

"Yeah! Come over here!" yelled one of the guitarists, and everyone laughed.

"Excellent!" Judge Jim joined in the laughter. "You two are in your final year, aren't you?" he said to a couple of the other singers. "Both Mr. Player and I feel you ought to have a solo slot each, using the backin' tracks you're used to."

That left just two older girls and Chloe, who was getting more and more worried about her own act.

"Right," said Mr. Player. "It's all coming together well. Now, you three ..." He looked thoughtful. "I don't think you'd make a good trio," he said to the older girls. "Chloe's voice is too different. It just wouldn't be a good fit." He was beginning to look a bit concerned. "How many acts have we decided on so far?" he asked the other teacher.

Judge Jim counted them out. "Two bands," he said,

"two solos, plus Rob and Ayesha's duet. That's five out of the six we need."

"Hmm," said Mr. Player while Chloe held her breath. If only they would let *her* sing solo. But then what would the other two girls do? And Mr. Player had just said that they wouldn't make a good trio. Trying to fit everyone into so few acts was turning into a nightmare.

"I know," said Judge Jim at last. Chloe and the others looked at him hopefully. "We have a vocalist for one of the bands, but not the other. How about lettin' Chloe sing with the second band?" he suggested. "Her voice is plenty strong enough. Then you two can sing a duet. Would that work for you?"

The two older girls looked relieved and so did Mr. Player.

"Good idea," he agreed.

Chloe was silent, but inside she was shouting, *What about me? What about what's right for me?* Chloe had never been a vocalist in a band before. Surely now wasn't the time to try something so different? She glanced over at the musicians and felt even more worried. She knew that most of them were into rock music, while she was a pop singer who was used to singing along to bright and breezy backing tracks. How would she cope with heavy guitar solos and earsplitting drums and cymbals?

This was supposed to be her big moment, but she was going to have to perform in a way she never had before. This wasn't how it was supposed to be.

No! Chloe wanted to shout out in protest. *I can't do it. I don't know how. It's not fair!* But she didn't say anything. What was the point? It had all been decided. She was the most junior singer, so of course the older ones should get first choice. Chloe tried her hardest to feel pleased for everyone, she really did. But she simply couldn't be happy for them.

She glanced over at Danny and caught his eye. He looked less happy than he had a few minutes ago. He was probably worrying about how Chloe was going to perform as part of a rock band.

"You'd better go to your classes now," said Judge Jim. "But try to get together with your fellow artists as soon as possible to discuss what you're goin' to perform. We'll give you all the help you need, and of course you'll have priority for rehearsal rooms. Go ahead. And good luck!"

As Chloe made her way toward the door, one of the guitarists grabbed her arm. It was Zil Gibson. She knew that Danny had always wanted to work with him, but Chloe had never thought she'd have to. "Hi," he said. "It looks as if you'll be with us. We're having a band meeting at lunchtime in the library. Is that okay with you?"

Chloe nodded numbly.

"Good," said Zil. "Don't be late, okay? Come right after the last class before lunch. We have a lot to talk about."

"Okay," agreed Chloe nervously.

She couldn't avoid walking to English with Danny because they had class together, but she didn't really want to talk.

"You all right?" he asked.

Chloe looked at him miserably. "No," she admitted.

"Not really. It's okay for you," she went on. "You're used to playing with other people. You'll fit in fine. But I won't. I thought it was going to be so great being a Rising Star, but it's nothing like I imagined. How am I going to learn to sing rock music in a band? I'm a *solo* artist. And I'm a pop singer, not a rocker."

"It'll be all right," Danny told her encouragingly. "Judge Jim thinks you can do it, right? It can't be *that* difficult."

"Judge Jim isn't my singing teacher, is he?" Chloe snapped. "And you're a drummer, so what do you know? It's not as easy as you think." She wanted to cry, but took refuge in being angry instead. "I should have known that you wouldn't understand." She hurried away from him before tears could start trickling down her face.

When she got to class the lesson had already started, so she didn't have to explain to the others what had happened.

On the way to the next class, though, Pop and Lolly wanted to hear how the meeting had gone. Chloe was noncommittal. She was trying to feel positive, but it wasn't easy.

"You must be so thrilled," Pop said. "It's such a cool thing to be a Rising Star."

"Ye-es," Chloe agreed. "But it's scary, too. There's a lot to think about."

"I don't know how you can *think* of singing with the boys," said Tara scathingly when she heard what had been decided. "*You're* not a rocker!" Tara played bass and was always trying to tell the others that rock was much cooler than pop. "You don't even have the right clothes," she added with a laugh.

"Don't be so horrible!" Lolly told Tara. "Don't pay attention to her, Chloe. Tara's only jealous. You'll be fine singing rock for a change. It'll be fun. The hardest part is over now that you've won your place. All you have to do is sing!"

Chloe gave her a tight smile. She longed to have some time alone with Lolly so she could tell her best friend how she really felt, but she'd have to wait until later in the day for that.

As the morning passed, Chloe began to calm down. She felt sorry that she'd snapped at Danny. He'd only been trying to help. And Judge Jim might not be her singing teacher, but he had tons of experience in the music industry. Besides, wouldn't Mr. Player have intervened if he'd thought she wasn't capable of singing with a band? He *was* her singing teacher and had been there while it was being discussed.

Maybe Chloe had overreacted, but she still wasn't happy. She didn't *want* to sing with a band. She didn't want the responsibility that came with it. She was happier on her own. However, she decided that if this was the way it had to be, she simply had to do her best.

At the end of morning classes, Chloe made her way to the meeting thinking hard. *It'll be a challenge,* she told herself, looking on the bright side. *And I won't let it beat me. Maybe it'll even be fun!*

3. Disaster

As soon as Chloe, Danny, and the others met in the library at lunchtime, Zil Gibson took control. "Let's see if we can make a few decisions right away," he said. "What type of songs do you like to perform, Chloe?" he asked.

"I always sing pop songs," she told him.

He grimaced and exchanged glances with the rest of the band. They looked totally unimpressed, while Danny avoided catching Chloe's eye. He was looking almost as worried as she felt.

"No way!" said Zil with a decided shake of his head. "We're into rock. We can't have a *pop* singer as our vocalist. Your stuff would be much too light for us. It would sound terrible."

28

"But—" said Chloe.

"You should be singing to a simple backing track, not performing with us," Zil told her.

"I know that," agreed Chloe miserably. "That's what I thought I'd be doing. But it's not my fault. I didn't ask to share an act with a group of rock musicians." Her heart sank. It had obviously been a mistake to think that this might be fun.

"That's true," agreed Danny, and Chloe looked at him gratefully. "So can't we make the best of it?" he went on. "Can't we come up with some kind of compromise?"

"But that would mean none of us would be able to perform the kind of music we like best!" protested Lenny Parsons, the rhythm guitarist.

"That's right," agreed Zil. "We don't want to play pop. Look, we outnumber you, Chloe. You'll just have to make the best of it."

"Um . . . I've got an idea," said Danny quickly.

Chloe felt close to tears. She looked at her friend anxiously, eager for any help he could give.

"Haven't you been working on a song that Charlie Owen's dad wrote?" Danny asked Chloe.

She nodded. "Yes. It's on their latest album. But I've been giving it a very different treatment."

"Now we're getting somewhere," said Zil a bit more enthusiastically. "What's the song?"

Chloe told them. "But when I sing it, it's a light ballad," she protested. "Mr. Player has changed the tempo and everything. I couldn't possibly sing it as a rock anthem."

"At least you know the words!" said Jeff Crocker, the band's bassist. "It's a good start. And if you like the song, you can't be *totally* antirock."

"I'm *not*," said Chloe. "It's just that I don't like the idea of singing the song that way."

"Can everyone get to a rehearsal after dinner?" said Zil, ignoring Chloe's last remark. "We need to have a run-through of the song as soon as possible. I can lend you a copy of the CD if you don't have one," he added to Chloe. "You'll need to listen to how the vocalist sings it, won't you?"

During dinner, Chloe tried to imagine herself singing the song as heavy rock, but the gentle arrangement Mr. Player had created for it was the one that filled her mind. She'd just have to hope the boys would tone down their version a little, and come up with something she could cope with.

Chloe didn't want to be late for her first rehearsal, but somehow her feet dragged as she made her way over to the Rock Department, where they had decided to meet. When she got there, the band was set up and jamming together. They were obviously getting along fine musically. It was impressive, because it was the first time they had all played as a band and they sounded good. But Chloe was completely excluded. All she could do was wait until they had finished the song they were playing.

"Great!" said Zil when the song came to an end.

"With a little work we'll be fine," agreed Lenny.

They all seemed pretty happy, but then Zil turned to Chloe, who was standing awkwardly nearby.

"You're late," he told her.

"Sorry," she mumbled.

"Why didn't you join in?" he said accusingly. "Don't you even know that song? We chose a very famous one so we could all try to get comfortable with each other."

"Sorry," she said again. "Yes, I do know it, but I wasn't sure if you wanted me to...sorry."

Danny was giving her a sympathetic smile, but Chloe couldn't return it. She felt terrible. She didn't have any problem with confidence when she was performing alone, but she couldn't possibly have simply marched in and started singing along with the boys. She had no idea that this was what they had expected her to do.

Nervously, she put her bag down and went up to a spare microphone mounted on a stand. While she fiddled with it to make the stand the right height for herself, the boys played a few riffs. Standing among all the amps and cables, Chloe could feel a little ripple of the excitement that went with electrified music, but it was far outweighed by her fear. She was used to a large, uncluttered space in which to sing, but here there were guitar leads to trip over and Danny's drums right behind her. The neck of Zil's guitar seemed worryingly close to Chloe's head and it moved around at the edge of her sight when he played. It was bound to ruin her concentration.

"Okay. Let's try your song, then," said Zil. "None of us have played it before, so don't expect perfection."

It's not my song, thought Chloe resentfully. *Don't blame me if you can't play it. I didn't choose it, did I?*

But there was no time to argue. Zil nodded at Danny to count them in and they were off.

Danny set a galloping pace and everyone had to scramble to keep up. After the first couple of bars he slowed down a little, but the tempo was still much faster than Chloe was used to singing the song at. It was true that she knew the lyrics really well, but she was unable to put any sort of feeling into her voice. It was simply a matter of getting the words out.

When they'd finished the song, there was a short silence. "Well, it's a start," said Zil in a resigned voice, unplugging his guitar. "I've got to go. Same time tomorrow?"

Everyone nodded and Chloe went to pick up her bag. As she was heading for the door, she heard Lenny speak to Danny.

"I thought you said she had an awesome voice," he said.

Chloe didn't wait for Danny's reply. She pushed the door open and ran out of the rehearsal room. How was she going to get through the next couple of weeks? She had dreamed of being a Rising Star for so long, but now the dream had turned into a horrible nightmare.

Mr. Player came to the next rehearsal. "I know you're just getting started," he said to the band afterward. "But...is that the song you all want to perform?"

"Yes," said Zil. "It has good opportunities for drum and guitar solos and Chloe already knew the words, so it made sense."

"Okay. I'll work on it with Chloe, then," he said without further comment.

But in spite of that, the next few rehearsals weren't much better and it seemed that even when the others made mistakes, Chloe still wasn't blameless.

"You're not acting like part of the team," Zil complained one day as everyone stopped playing once again when Chloe faltered.

"I'm trying to," said Chloe, close to tears. "But I'm not used to performing with other people. And you skipped the chorus just now! What am I supposed to do when that happens?"

Zil sighed. "You're not supposed to just stop! I agree that it wasn't your fault, but when things go wrong you have to improvise. You can't simply stop singing and look confused. We all have to cover for each other when we make mistakes. If *you* forgot your words, I'd probably repeat the riff a couple of times until you got yourself together." He looked at his watch. "Okay. We'd better finish now. Same time tomorrow?"

"Sure." Danny nodded and put down his drumsticks. Jeff and Lenny looked at each other.

"We're not happy with the way things are going," said Lenny awkwardly.

"Yeah," agreed Jeff. "If we're not careful, we'll run out of time. We've got to get this right, and if Chloe can't gel with us, we're in big trouble. I mean, we've toned down the heavy rock style, but Chloe's voice still isn't really working."

Chloe waited anxiously to hear what Zil had to say. He was the oldest, and very much in charge, but however hurtful Jeff's comments were, Chloe knew in her heart that he and Lenny were right. At the moment she *was* holding them back.

Zil didn't look at Chloe. "Don't worry," he said to the boys. "It'll be fine. We'll get it together. And if we don't, as a last resort we can always perform it as an instrumental."

Jeff and Lenny looked relieved, but Chloe was appalled. *Do it without a singer? No!* She just *had* to get this right, otherwise she'd be out of the Rising Stars Concert! Chloe knew that the teachers wouldn't let her jeopardize the others' chance and there was no alternative act she could join. She *had* to make this work or lose the opportunity to perform on television.

Chloe went to her singing lesson later that day very downhearted indeed, but Mr. Player was more upbeat about the situation when she told him about it.

"Remember how determined you were to get a place at this school," he said. "You didn't let yourself give up then when the odds were against you and you shouldn't give up now. You can do this, Chloe. I'm sure you can. It's just a shame that you've chosen to use a song you've already learned as a ballad."

"*I* didn't choose it," Chloe told him. "Danny mentioned that I'd been learning it, and they decided it would be best. I couldn't suggest anything else because I didn't know their favorite songs."

"Oh dear," said Mr. Player sympathetically. "That is a shame. If they'd chosen a song that was new to you, you might have found it a bit easier. You just have to keep at it. It'll come in the end. And I know you prefer pop, but your voice is ideal for rock, too, you know. Get some of that awesome power going and you'll be quite a rock chick!" He smiled kindly at her and she tried to smile back, but her mouth turned down and she couldn't manage it.

"Wanting to sing the song as a ballad is part of it," she agreed. "I really prefer your arrangement of the song. But it's more than that," she admitted. "I know where I am, singing to the backing track you made on the keyboard. I know every note of every instrument you've put on there inside out. I can do what I want with my voice and the track is always the same. But with four other people playing live, it's so unpredictable. When the others make mistakes, I can't handle it and I know I'm letting them all down."

"It's good to be a perfectionist," Mr. Player told her. "But finding perfection in a band means thinking on your feet and adapting to what is happening around you. With five people performing together, the song is bound to be slightly different each time."

"But I *hate* that," protested Chloe. "It feels wrong."

"Well, I've been teaching you how to make a song as perfect as it can be, but you know yourself that no two performances are *exactly* the same. Everyone makes mistakes, and with enough practice you can learn to cover for each other."

"I suppose," said Chloe. She bit her lip. "I'm so stupid."

"No, you're not," said Mr. Player. "You're just used to your way of doing things and now you have four other people to consider." He smiled at her. "You know, there are lots of artists who would never think of singing to a backing track. Yes, it's very safe, but compared to a band it can be rather mechanical. It takes a lot of rehearsing together, but when you sing with musicians you trust, you can really let go and the whole performance will fly!" He smiled sympathetically at Chloe's doubtful expression. "When's your next rehearsal?" he asked.

Chloe told him and he looked in his day planner. "I'll come along again and see what I can do to help," he offered. "You do realize you're very young to be chosen as a Rising Star, don't you?"

"I guess so," said Chloe again. It had been exciting

to be named as a Rising Star, but since then she had spent every day wondering if she was capable of living up to the title.

"The problem with this concert is that we try to shoehorn so many students in," said Mr. Player. "Usually the singers are no problem, because we can easily have several performing the same song, taking a verse each. But your voice is so powerful and so different, we couldn't do that with you, and at the same time we really had to let the older ones have the solo spots. If you feel you can't cope with singing with the band, there would be no shame in bowing out this time." He noticed her horrified expression. "You'll be a Rising Star again in the future," he reassured her. "I'm sure of it. This isn't going to be your only chance."

Chloe shook her head fiercely. "But I *want* to do it this time," she told him. "I can't give up now!"

"Even though rock isn't really your thing, and even though you're not happy being a member of a band?"

Chloe looked stubbornly back at him. "It's all singing," she told him. "I *should* be able to do it." She felt fierce and determined, but then the fight went out of her. What if she *couldn't* make this treatment of the song really fly, or feel comfortable performing with others? She'd be letting the boys down and that would be terrible.

"I'll give it a few more days," she told Mr. Player. "But I don't want to ruin things for the band. If I can't get it soon I... I'll have to give up." She nearly burst into tears as she said it, but Chloe knew it was the right thing to say. She couldn't ruin the boys' big moment.

"That's very brave, Chloe," acknowledged Mr. Player. "But I don't think it will come to that. You know, I think if you could just relax with the band, you'd be fine."

"You might be right," said Chloe miserably. "I'll try."

"That's the right attitude," agreed Mr. Player. "Now listen. I've got a suggestion for you."

"What?" asked Chloe, sure it would be something else she would make a mess of.

"Charlie Owen's dad has given Judge Jim some backstage passes for his next gig," Mr. Player told her.

"It's tomorrow night. And because you're going to be singing one of his band's songs at the Rising Stars Concert, we thought we'd offer them to you and your fellow band members. Maybe watching the band perform the song you're covering might help you to see beyond our version of it. I'm sure you'll like their performance, even though you're not much of a rock fan. Have you ever seen any really big stars perform live?"

Chloe shook her head. "No," she admitted.

"Well, now is your chance," said Mr. Player. "And not only will you see them perform, with luck, you'll be able to meet them as well. I think it's an opportunity you should definitely take. It will be good for the band to spend some time together away from rehearsals, as well. It could be just the boost you need."

Chloe couldn't help feeling a little excited about this, in spite of her worries about her own concert. Charlie Owen was in her grade, and his dad was in a mega-famous band. Maybe it *would* help to see them play live. At any rate, it couldn't do any harm.

"How many people are going from school?" she asked, wondering if Pop and Lolly would get a chance to go, too. It would be nice to be able to sit with friends.

"I'm not sure how many passes we have," said Mr. Player, "but I don't suppose it is very many. Judge Jim is going to take the minibus, so there won't be hordes of you. I think Charlie will go, though, and maybe there will be enough tickets for him to take a friend."

It was reassuring to know that Judge Jim was going to take them. Chloe liked him a lot. She was sure Danny would go, too. He would *never* pass up such an amazing opportunity. "All right," she told Mr. Player. "I'll go."

"Good." He smiled. "I'm sure you won't regret it. I'll tell Judge Jim. Watch how the lead singer interacts with his fellow band members, but most of all just enjoy hanging out with *your* band as well as a famous one."

"I will," Chloe promised.

4. An Evening to Remember

"It's not fair," said Tara the following night as Chloe got ready to go out with her fellow band members. "I'd love to meet my favorite bassist and see him play. The pass will be wasted on you."

"I hope not," said Chloe, putting on her best pair of jeans and brushing her hair. "I'm sorry you can't go, but Mr. Player thought it was a good idea for me to be there."

"Huh!" said Tara, still looking very disgruntled.

Chloe piled into the minibus with all the boys. She wished Lolly had been able to go. As that wasn't possible, Chloe would have liked to sit with Danny, but he was deep in conversation with Zil and so Chloe found herself sitting alone.

So much for hanging out with her band. But it wasn't too bad. Judge Jim played some cool music, and the ride wasn't very long.

Soon they were nearing the arena where the gig was going to take place. Chloe and the others waited impatiently while Judge Jim found a good spot to park and then they all climbed out of the minibus.

"It's huge!" Chloe breathed in awe as she stared at the building in front of them.

"Dad's played bigger venues than this," Charlie told her. "Some of the other places are twice this size."

Chloe simply couldn't imagine anything much bigger than this enormous building.

"One day you'll all have enough fans to fill a stadium like this," said Judge Jim, feeling in his pocket for the backstage passes and handing them out. The passes were large plastic rectangles with the word BACKSTAGE printed in big, black letters. They were clipped onto long green cords, which everyone hung around their necks. Chloe put hers on, feeling very important. Danny glanced at Chloe and they exchanged grins. This was *so* exciting.

Judge Jim took the students to a small side door and knocked. It opened a few inches and a face framed with long dreadlocks peered out. When its owner saw Jim, he opened the door wide and engulfed the teacher in a huge bear hug.

"Good to see you, man!" the guy said, standing back and looking at Judge Jim with a broad grin on his face. "It's been too long." Then he caught sight of the students standing awkwardly outside. "Hi, Charlie," he said, and smiled at the others. "Come on in, all of you. We've been expecting you."

"Dag is one of Dad's roadies," explained Charlie as they followed the man along a brightly lit corridor to the band's dressing room.

Chloe and the others filed shyly into the room. There wasn't a lot of space. There were clothes and guitars, plates, bottles, and cans littered over every available surface. It was just as Chloe had always imagined backstage chaos to be.

She recognized a big man who was waving at them as Abe, the lead singer. She also recognized Charlie's father, from when he'd picked up Charlie at the end of last semester. In fact, the band members were so well known that she recognized all of them immediately.

Abe tossed some clothes off chairs into a heap so that a few of the students could sit down. Charlie was in his element, showing off to his friends about how close he was to these megastars. But he shouldn't have bothered—Chloe was totally impressed anyway!

Soon Judge Jim was chatting with the lead guitarist while Charlie and Danny were talking to Charlie's dad about drums. Lenny, Jeff, and Stew, Charlie's friend, were talking to the other musicians, but Chloe felt too shy to join in. She stared at a huge bowl of mangoes on the dressing table. Her initial excitement was draining away and she began to wonder if it would have been better if she hadn't come.

"Would you like one?"

Chloe looked up to see Abe towering over her. He was smiling, but Chloe found him a bit scary. He was so big and so famous. She didn't know what to say.

"A mango," Abe elaborated. "Would you like one? I always have one before I sing. Seems to lubricate my throat. Hang on." He picked up several mangoes and gave them to a man who had been hanging out in the room. Chloe didn't recognize him. "Can we get these done now?" Abe asked. The man nodded.

"So what do you play?" he added to Chloe.

"I don't," Chloe admitted. "I'm a singer, but I don't usually—"

Abe cut her off. "Me, too!" he said, as if she might not have realized. He waved his arm over to where Judge Jim was still deep in conversation. "Ol' Jim and I gigged together until he decided to give it all up and teach," he told her. "Then I took up with these guys a few years ago. You've got one cool teacher there," he added admiringly. "What he does for young people is amazing!"

"I know," agreed Chloe.

"John Owen was telling me about this concert thing you do on TV. His boy Charlie didn't get chosen this time, but you kids did. That right?"

Chloe explained all about the Rising Stars Concert. Abe seemed impressed when she told him they were going to be singing one of the band's songs.

"Wow. That's really cool," he said. "I hope it goes well for you. I've had some real fun with that song. You can do so much with it."

"Yes," Chloe replied doubtfully. Abe was easy to talk to, and she felt the urge to confess her problems with singing in a band to him, in case he had any suggestions. But just then the man came back with drinks and the mangoes and the moment was lost.

Soon it would be time for the concert to start, and after they'd had their drinks, Judge Jim shepherded the students from the room.

"See you at the end," called Charlie's dad as they left.

Chloe and the others had fantastic seats, almost in

the front. When Chloe looked behind her, the arena seemed to stretch away forever. To the people in the very back of the vast stadium, the band would look like tiny dolls. But there were two huge screens showing the concert as well, so at least those people would be able to see something.

The whole place erupted into deafening applause when the band finally came onstage. They swung right into a song, and the audience went berserk at the first couple of chords. Chloe was forced to put her hands over her ears for a few minutes until they'd calmed down a little.

To begin with, Chloe was enjoying the atmosphere so much that she forgot she was supposed to be studying the band's technique. But once she stopped gazing around at the lights, the backdrop, and the huge arena, she began to notice little communications between the band members. Sometimes it was just a slight nod from one to another that she would have missed if she'd been farther away. Then she realized that in one song someone had made a bad mistake.

The lead guitarist turned to Abe and laughed. Abe grinned and sang the same line again and then the song went on as if nothing had happened. It *was* possible to make mistakes and still move on.

Chloe and the others were soon lost in the fantastic performance. Chloe even forgot that she knew the performers because she was so totally caught up in the sights and sounds in front of her. It was much better than watching concerts on television. The energy coming off the stage was like a living thing, and it was feeding off the audience. She had never seen or felt anything like it before in her life. Chloe realized that Mr. Player had been right. When a singer and musicians really got it together, the performance *did* fly. If only she and the boys could do the same.

After a few songs, Abe spoke to the audience. It gave the other band members a chance to grab a drink. Chloe could see Charlie's dad wiping his hands and drumsticks with a towel before he reached for his water bottle. Then Abe mentioned his good friend Judge Jim and, to Chloe's amazement, a spotlight snaked its way off the stage and shone briefly onto Judge Jim, who was sitting next to her. He raised his hand good-naturedly and the audience cheered. It was obvious that lots of them had heard of Judge Jim Henson.

For a moment, some of the spotlight shone onto Chloe as well. The bright white light illuminated one half of her body while the other half stayed dark. Part of Chloe longed for the whole spotlight to fall on her. It made her want to perform. She would have loved to have gone up there onstage in front of such an amazing audience.

Then she realized. This was what had been lacking in her rehearsals with the Rising Stars band. Only half of her had wanted to rehearse. The other half was still scared of being forced to sing in a way that didn't come naturally. But it was no good performing halfheartedly. You had to throw yourself completely into it or not at all. Yes, she'd been working very hard on the song, but her lack of trust in the others had stopped her from relaxing into the music so that she could really feel it. And singing rock music could be exciting, she saw that, especially with the song the band was performing now. It was one she hadn't heard before, but she could see herself up there onstage doing justice to *this* song! If only she could do that with the song they'd chosen.

Chloe decided to be brave. She would really go for it. She had nothing to lose. She would make herself be a *real* member of the band, not a reluctant singer who didn't fit in. So what if she made mistakes? The others did and didn't beat themselves up about it. They just kept on going and did it better next time. She had to find the same confidence, and trust that everything would work out if they kept trying.

I will succeed, she told herself. *I will!*

5. Breakthrough

Backstage after the performance, there was a mass of people all talking in loud, excited voices. Judge Jim got Chloe and the boys through the crush with difficulty and eventually they managed to reach the dressing room. Here, it was almost as chaotic as in the hallway. Judge Jim handed Charlie and his friend Stew over to Charlie's dad. The boys were catching a ride in the band's tour bus and going to Charlie's home for the weekend.

"You were fantastic!" said Chloe to Abe when she found herself near him.

"Wasn't I?" he said, with a twinkle in his eye. "Glad you enjoyed it," he added more seriously. "I hope your concert goes well. I'll try to catch it on TV if I can. Just relax and get into the groove. Yeah, Dag!" he yelled over her head. "I'm coming."

By the time the students were getting into their minibus, people were streaming out of the arena.

The four remaining boys couldn't stop chattering to one another, and Chloe almost sat back down where she had been on the journey there, but she didn't want to be alone.

Before she could lose her nerve, she joined the boys. It was tricky butting in when the boys were still excited about the concert. Apart from a friendly smile from Danny, the others were too involved with their conversation to acknowledge her.

"And that riff on the last song was just phenomenal!" Zil was saying.

"I think the drummer had the edge on you, Danny!" teased Jeff.

Danny grinned. "Maybe just a little," he agreed. "Hey, Chloe! What did *you* think of it?" he asked.

Suddenly they were all waiting to hear what she had

to say and Chloe wondered desperately if it had been a good idea to try to push her way in. In the end, she simply told them what she thought.

"Well," she said, "I enjoyed it much more than I thought I would. They are one cool band, especially Abe."

"Yes?" said Zil.

"And I really liked that song near the end," she continued shyly, encouraged that he seemed genuinely interested in what she had to say. "You know the one. 'Summer Lightning,' I think it was called."

"Oh, yeah! That's a *great* song," agreed Lenny.

Danny started beating out the thumping intro and Jeff made the sound of the heavy bass. Grinning, Zil and Lenny came in on their imagined guitars, Lenny's plaintive whine under Zil's lead. If this was the real band, Abe would come in now with his howling lyrics.

Relax and get into the groove, he'd told her, and for the first time she felt that maybe she could. It had been such a great night, and everyone was happy. If she was ever going to gel with the band, it was now.

As she sang the first line, Zil and the others faltered with surprise. But Danny kept the beat going, slapping his hands on his jeans, the back of the seat, anywhere that was available.

The others soon recovered, and by the time they got to the chorus they were in complete harmony. Zil abandoned his imaginary guitar lead to sing the two-line chorus with Chloe and then picked up where he'd left off.

Chloe belted out the rest of the song, singing just the notes for which she couldn't remember the lyrics. By the end she was out of breath, but one look at the boys' faces told her that they were as pleased as she was. Danny bashed out the rhythm for another song and they were off again.

By the time the minibus arrived back at Rockley Park, Chloe was happier than she had been for ages. She felt as if she'd made a huge breakthrough. Their enjoyment of the concert had united them all and their different ages, abilities, and musical preferences didn't seem to matter so much now.

It was very late, but the summer-night air was still quite warm. Judge Jim had driven the minibus right up to the door of the girls' dorm, but Chloe paused before she got off.

"That song," she said to the boys. "The one we sang first tonight. Can we try it for real tomorrow?"

"'Summer Lightning?'" asked Zil. "You'd rather do that than the one you know?"

Chloe nodded. "I realize there isn't much time, but I think we could really make it our own. I felt . . ." She blushed uncomfortably. "Inspired. . . you know?"

Danny nodded. "I know," he said. "Okay, so we didn't have our instruments with us, but Chloe's right. I think we could do great things with that song. It wouldn't just be a simple cover. For a start, Chloe's voice does things Abe's doesn't."

"That's true!" said Zil with a laugh.

"Your voice was awesome," said Jeff. "Especially when you skimmed over those words."

"That was because I couldn't remember them!" Chloe admitted.

"Well, it was still awesome," Jeff insisted. "If you can do that at the concert, it'll be so cool."

"Can you have your band meetin' in the morning instead of now?" complained Judge Jim with a wry smile. "It's really late and I want to get home!"

"Sorry!" said Chloe, and she jumped off the bus so he could take the boys back to their dorm. When she turned to wave good night, Judge Jim gave her a grin and lowered his window.

"Reckon tonight has been a success in more ways than one," he told her through the open window.

"I guess it has," she agreed. "Thank you for taking us on such an incredible trip."

Chloe crept upstairs and into her room. The light was off and she thought everyone was asleep, but as she got into bed, Pop sat up.

"Did you have a good time?"

"Yes," said Chloe. "It was amazing."

Soon, the light was on and all three girls were listening to Chloe's description of the evening.

"Was the bassist playing his old Fender Precision?" asked Tara.

"Um. . . I don't know," admitted Chloe. "Sorry. It was a red guitar. That's all I remember."

"Huh!" snorted Tara. "Typical! Singers *never* notice instruments."

"Do you know what the best part of the whole evening was?" Chloe went on, ignoring Tara's comment. "Coming back on the bus we were singing and stuff, and we all got along really well. I felt totally relaxed with the boys for the first time since we've been rehearsing together. It was great! We're going to try a different song tomorrow and I think it might just work!"

"That's wonderful," said Lolly. "I know how worried you've been about the concert, but maybe you'll be all right now."

"Don't get too relaxed or you'll make mistakes," Tara warned darkly.

"That's not very helpful," Pop complained. "Just as Chloe is starting to feel a little better."

"Well, I *think* I am, but I still need all the help I can get," said Chloe. "So what do *you* think the key is to gelling with them if it's not relaxing? You should know, Tara. You play in a band."

Tara sniffed. "It's not relaxing. Or at least not totally," she said. "That's part of it, but the most important thing is trust. You have to trust that everyone else is with you and that they'll back you up whatever happens. That way, you're free to perform at your best."

Chloe nodded. "Yes," she agreed. "I think maybe you're right."

"Of course I am," said Tara. "I bet you find it hard to trust Zil and the others because you don't know them very well and you aren't totally convinced they know what they're doing. Isn't that right?"

"Yes, I guess so," agreed Chloe. "They all make mistakes but somehow they just keep on going, and I find it hard to do that. I trust Danny, though," she added.

"But you need to trust them *all*, or the whole thing falls apart," Tara explained.

"I suppose," Chloe mused.

"And there's another thing," added Tara, yawning hugely. "Just as important."

"What?"

"They have to trust *you*," she said.

"Yes," Chloe agreed slowly, biting her lip. "They do, don't they?"

Over the next few days, every member of the band made a huge effort. Choosing a new song had been a really good idea and Chloe had taken Tara's advice to heart and worked hard to gain their trust. Now, at last, they were really working as a team and things started to improve dramatically. When Judge Jim dropped in on a rehearsal, he was very pleased at their progress.

"Good job, all of you," he said with a smile in Chloe's direction. "You're really beginnin' to rock. You spendin' much time together out of rehearsals?"

"I was going to suggest that we all have our meals together from now until the concert," said Zil.

"The more you can act like family, the better," Judge

Jim told them approvingly. "Zil's idea is good. You get inside each other's head and you'll perform amazingly. If I were you, I'd go for it."

One evening, shortly before the big day, Judge Jim and Mr. Player got all the Rising Stars performers together so they could watch a recording of last year's performances.

"If you know what to expect, it might calm your nerves a little," said Mr. Player. "Of course, this is the finished recording, and the shots you will see of the individual performers were taken during the day and edited in later, but it will give you an idea of the set and the way you'll be presented."

They all watched as the DVD played. Afterward, there were lots of comments.

"It was *so* slick," said Zil.

"And everyone looked so *glamorous!*" Chloe added admiringly.

"It *is* slick," said Mr. Player. "But you're all professionals and will do very well. Every one of you is more than capable of producing performances just as good as last year's stars."

"I hope so," said Danny fervently.

"And as for looking glamorous, the TV company is very good at making the students look fantastic," he added.

"So we don't get to decide what to wear?" asked Isla, looking rather disappointed.

"You do," said Mr. Player. "But then their wardrobe department looks at you and makes suggestions. Sometimes clothes that look great in real life can look very different on television."

"Someone told me that television can make you look fatter," said Zil.

"I thought it was thinner," said Chloe.

"Well, whichever it is, you don't need to worry," said Mr. Player. "By the time wardrobe and makeup have finished with you, you'll all look wonderful. Just wear whatever you're comfortable in, and they'll do the rest."

✳

But when Chloe reported back to Pop and Lolly, they wanted to get involved in what she was going to wear.

"Come on," said Pop. "We're professional models. Look at all the things we've got that you can borrow." She threw open her closet door dramatically. She was right, of course. She and Lolly had been given lots of cool clothes by famous designers. And the twins were very generous with them.

"We might as well make an effort with what you wear," said Lolly. "It'll be fun."

"Why not layer your red dress with my silk shirt? That would look cute," suggested Pop.

"Yes, it might work. Come on," Lolly urged, opening her closet door as well. "The studio people will have their own ideas, but we should definitely send you off looking your best."

"All right," Chloe agreed. "Maybe doing that will take my mind off being nervous."

"You don't need to be nervous," said Pop. "You'll be fine now that you and the band have gelled."

"We're not free and clear yet," admitted Chloe. "The

new song is better, but Lenny is having trouble with his riff. It's a really tricky one. And because it leads into Zil's solo, Zil can come unstuck, too."

"It'll be fine on the day," said Pop. "I'm sure it will. Zil and Lenny will figure it out."

"I hope so," said Chloe. "Because if they don't, *I'm* very likely to go wrong, too!"

6. Concert Day

On the evening before the Rising Stars Concert, Chloe tried to keep herself busy so she wouldn't have time to be too nervous. She finished all her homework, even parts that didn't need handing in right away, and played Ping-Pong with Pop for ages, but nothing could keep her from thinking of the big day.

Even so, Lolly was the first to spy the letter on Chloe's bed that night.

"What is it?" asked Pop as Chloe opened the envelope.

"It's a letter from the principal," said Chloe in surprise. She scanned it quickly and then read it out loud: "'On behalf of the staff, I would like to wish you good luck for the Rising Stars Concert tomorrow. You have worked very hard to get this far and I hear great things about the act you have prepared. I hope everything goes well for you and that you enjoy the day. Best wishes, Mrs. Janet Sharkey.'"

"I didn't know the principal's name was Janet," said Pop with a giggle.

"What a nice letter," said Lolly.

"She wants to encourage you so you don't let the school down," growled Tara.

Chloe put the letter back in the envelope. She would keep it forever. If she never did anything else, at least she had this to prove that she'd been a Rising Star in her first year at Rockley Park. And that was really something to be proud of!

When it was lights-out, Chloe didn't want to keep on talking like the girls usually did. She wanted a few minutes alone with her thoughts before she went to sleep . . . if she could actually *get* to sleep.

She lay down and felt the envelope crackle under

her pillow. Mrs. Sharkey had heard "great things" about their act!

Rock would never be Chloe's favorite sort of music, but she had really gotten into the band and was thoroughly enjoying singing like a rocker for a change. It was fun, and she hoped that the fun would shine through in her performance.

The boys were great musicians. And they had given the song a more lighthearted feel to complement Chloe's approach. She hoped it worked. They all thought it did and it seemed the teachers did, too. If only Lenny could get his riff right. That was the scariest thing, because if he couldn't, Chloe wasn't sure that she would be able to go on without faltering. Everything hinged on that.

Chloe tried to get to sleep but the riff was going around and around in her head, keeping her awake. If Lenny did falter, Chloe hoped with all her heart that she'd be able to keep on, that she wouldn't let the band down. She turned over and sighed. It would all be over by this time tomorrow.

The envelope crackled under her pillow once more, but she didn't hear it. At last, she had fallen asleep.

In the morning, Chloe was up early. She washed her hair, and Pop dried it for her and put some wax in it.

"There!" said Pop, standing back and looking at Chloe with satisfaction. "Your hair looks really cool and it should stay that way all day. That's one less thing to worry about."

"Thanks, Pop," said Chloe.

"Break a leg," said Lolly when it was time to go. "We'll be thinking of you. I'm sure you'll have a terrific time." She gave her a hug and Pop joined in.

"I'm really jealous," Pop told her. "But you deserve your place, so enjoy!"

Chloe had been told to have her performance clothes in a bag and to wear something comfortable for rehearsals during the day, so she was in her usual jeans and T-shirt as she reached the main school building to wait for the minibus that was taking them to the studio. Several of the other Rising Stars students were there already and Chloe joined them, her face pale with mingled fear and excitement.

"Did you manage to eat any breakfast?" asked Zil, who was usually totally unflappable.

"No," admitted Chloe. "I couldn't."

"Me neither," Zil confessed. "But I brought a banana with me in case I get hungry on the bus."

"I didn't think it was a very long ride," said Chloe.

"It isn't," he said. "I don't know why I bothered really. It's just nerves, I guess. I've been trying to make sure I don't forget anything and a banana seemed like a good idea, but I'm sure they'll feed us!" He laughed. "I think I'm even more nervous now than I was when I came for my audition to get into this school."

"Oh. I hope I'm never *that* nervous again," said Chloe, and she immediately began to feel a little better.

Judge Jim and Mr. Player pulled up in the bus.

"We'll be with you every step of the way," Mr. Player told the students as they loaded their instruments. "So if you have any worries or problems, we'll be there to help."

"Where's Danny?" asked Judge Jim.

"I don't know," said Lenny. "He was in the Rock Department when I was collecting my guitar. I thought he was on his way."

Judge Jim looked at his watch. "I wouldn't have thought Danny would be the one to hold us up," he said. Zil and Lenny exchanged glances, and Chloe felt her stomach beginning to knot. Surely things weren't going to go wrong before they'd even left for the studio!

But then one of the older girls said, "Isn't that him?"

To everyone's relief, Danny was jogging along the path clutching his backpack. "Sorry," he puffed when he reached them. "I just realized that I had my most worn-out drumsticks with me instead of my best ones and I had to go back for them. You're sure I don't need to take my drum set, aren't you?" he added to Judge Jim.

"Don't worry," the teacher replied. "The studio set is really good and it'll be ready for you. All you need are your sticks."

Chloe gave her friend a sympathetic smile. Even

Danny, one of the calmest people she knew, must be feeling the tension.

The television studios were in the next town, which was only a short drive away. When the Rising Stars students arrived, they lugged their instruments into the reception area. They didn't have long to wait. A friendly-looking girl came through the swinging doors and approached them.

"Hi, I'm Julie," she said, shaking Judge Jim's hand and then Mr. Player's. "I'm the researcher for the program and will be looking after you today. If there's anything you need, just ask me and I'll do my best to help." She smiled at them all, and Chloe felt encouraged. It wasn't as scary here as she'd feared it might be.

Julie led the students down a hallway and into a large room with a table and chairs at one end. Several amps were already plugged in, and there was a simple drum set, too. "This is your rehearsal room," she told them. "You should all have time for at least one run-through here before you go down to do your sound checks in the studio. Sam will be here in a while to film some informal shots of you all. They will be edited into the final program between your acts to add interest for the viewers," she explained. "Drinks and cookies are there, and we'll be bringing in some light snacks for lunch. Oh, and later I'll be asking for some interesting snippets of information about each of you for the voice-over."

Chloe wondered what sort of information Julie would want. She couldn't think of anything interesting she'd done before today. Then she told herself not to worry. There were more important things to think about, like concentrating on making her performance the best she could. To do that, she would need to keep her energy levels up, so she went with the boys to investigate the cookies. She and Zil ate one each and Chloe began to feel a little more relaxed. The producer came to see them and, with the teachers' help, worked out the order in which they would perform.

"I'm glad we're not on first," Chloe whispered to

Danny when Judge Jim announced the running order. "Third is just about perfect."

Sam the cameraman showed up as well.

"I need to get some general shots of everyone chatting and rehearsing, and then some individual ones, too," he explained. "The audience today won't see any of the film, but afterward the recorded performances will be edited together with the shots I take and a voice-over will be scripted for the program."

"When will the program air?" asked Danny.

"It's usually shown as a Christmas special," said Sam.

"That's a long time away," said Chloe in disappointment. She'd been hoping to watch it with her family and friends over the summer break.

"That's TV for you." Sam smiled. "The school will get a copy of the program well before it goes out, so I think you'll get to see it very soon. But you should be pleased! Winter programs get a lot more viewers than summer ones. Haven't you noticed that they show a lot of repeats over the summer?"

Sam busied himself checking his camera, and Danny and Chloe exchanged glances. Chloe couldn't help being excited. The program might not be seen for absolutely forever, but it would *eventually* be shown and they were here now, in a TV studio! *That* was what really mattered. Then she thought about their song. No . . . what *really* mattered was for them to perform at their best. Suddenly all her doubts came flooding back, and her stomach did an enormous flip. They had to make the song perfect. It seemed impossible, but they simply *had to*.

7. An Exciting Time

At first, it was really difficult being filmed by Sam. He wanted lots of natural shots of the students, but with all the excitement in the air, it was very hard not to giggle when he pointed his camera in their direction. Danny dropped half a cookie into his drink by accident and everyone went into hysterics. They couldn't stop laughing for a while. But Sam was very patient, and eventually the students stopped being self-conscious and learned to ignore the camera.

When the first band got their instruments out and began to rehearse, everyone became much more businesslike. It might be a lot of fun being at a TV studio, but they had work to do and it would be a relief to get on with the job. Chloe and the rest of her band waited impatiently until it was their turn to do a run-through. Chloe was feeling really jittery now and there were still several hours to go until the audience would arrive. She was sure she'd feel better once she had a microphone in her hand, and she heaved a sigh of relief when it was their turn to rehearse.

But it wasn't that easy. Jeff made a bad mistake during their song, then Lenny faltered, and finally Zil made everything worse by swearing at them. Chloe and Danny plowed on as they had agreed they would if there was a problem, but there were an uncomfortable few seconds until the others picked up the song again. Everyone was thoroughly unsettled and Zil was mortified at having been recorded being rude to his fellow band members!

"I'm really sorry," he said. "I think the pressure must be getting to me."

"Don't worry," said Sam, still wielding his camera. "I'm sure it'll be edited out!"

Chloe was concerned that their bad rehearsal would

be included in the television program, but Judge Jim reassured her.

"Don't worry," he said. "They'll be lookin' for the human angle, not trying to make you look bad. The finished program will be mostly for people who don't know much about the music business. It'll be interestin' for them to see you workin' on the song and then performin' it perfectly during the concert."

"If we *do* manage to perform it perfectly," muttered Jeff anxiously.

The tension was getting to them all. Sam and the television company were only interested in what made good television, but the students knew that *their* purpose was to impress the small studio audience of experts. The students wanted recognition from the people who mattered.

Nobody managed to eat much of the pizza that was brought in for lunch, and when it was time for the students to change into the clothes they'd brought for their performances, Chloe felt very sick.

"I never thought I'd earn a place, did you?" said Ayesha, the girl who was going to be singing with Rob Copeland.

"No," Chloe replied. She struggled into the tight jeans Pop and Lolly had eventually decided she should wear and put on her sparkly green sleeveless top. "I hoped I might when I was higher up in the school, but never thought I would at the end of my first year."

"Well, I'm sure they don't choose people unless they think they can pull it off," Ayesha told her. "After all, this is a showcase for the school's talent. They wouldn't let us perform on television if they were afraid we'd let them down."

"I guess," agreed Chloe, but she wasn't sure of anything anymore. And her stomach was churning *so* badly.

Then Julie wanted to interview Chloe. The researcher needed some background material so that there'd be some interesting facts for the voice-over, which would accompany the shots taken of Chloe during rehearsal. Julie wanted to know how old Chloe was, how long she'd been at Rockley Park, and who her favorite singers were.

"Goodness! You're very young to be on the program," Julie said when Chloe gave her age. "Most of the performers are quite a bit older, but we have two young ones this year, right? Isn't one of the drummers almost the same age as you?"

"Yes," agreed Chloe. "And we both came from the same school and got scholarships to Rockley Park at the same time, too."

Julie was very pleased to hear this. "That's just the sort of thing we like to know," she said, writing it all down.

Next, everyone took turns visiting the makeup department. Even the boys had to have their faces powdered to stop them from shining under the strong studio lights. Then they each went to the wardrobe department.

Vicky, the wardrobe mistress, gave Chloe an encouraging smile. "That looks cute," she told her, "but I think we can find something to finish off the look."

She had a few words with her assistant, who brought out a wonderful, military-style jacket. It wasn't the kind of thing Chloe would have worn normally, but it made her feel trendy. When she joined Danny and the rest of the band, she found that the military theme had been subtly extended to the boys, too. The wardrobe department had been very clever in giving the band an identity without making it obvious. Danny was wearing a military-looking hat.

"Wow!" exclaimed Chloe when she saw him. "You look great."

Danny looked uncomfortable. "I didn't really want to wear it," he told her. "But Judge Jim said I should."

"You look awesome!" Chloe assured him.

"Do you think so?" said Danny, sounding relieved.

Time was ticking by, and it wasn't long before the whole group of teachers and students was taken to see the studio where they would perform. Chloe had never seen a place like this before. It was huge, but the actual performance space was much smaller than she had imagined.

"It's like a stage set without a stage!" Chloe said to Danny in surprise.

The walls of the enormous room were painted flat black, as were the floor and the ceiling. The ceiling was very high and filled with lots of lights, only a few of which were switched on. In the middle of the room was a circle of white floor with several white screens obscuring the black walls behind them.

"This is where you'll perform," said Julie, pointing at the white circle of floor.

"It's very small," said Danny anxiously.

"Don't worry," said Julie. "Everything fits in okay. We've done this type of concert lots of times. And you'll get the chance for a run-through in a few minutes. You'll feel more comfortable once you've done that."

"I like the sign," said Ayesha.

"Me, too," agreed Chloe. In the middle of the center screen was the huge sparkly star she remembered from watching last year's concert. ROCKLEY'S RISING STARS was in glittery writing inside the star. The students would be standing right in front of it when they performed.

"I thought there would be a much bigger audience," said Zil, looking at the rows of chairs facing the Rising Stars sign.

Mr. Player shook his head. "Television can play lots of tricks," he said. "It's a small invited audience, but when the concert is shown on TV, it will look as if you are playing in a very large venue."

Chloe had been going to ask why the room had to be so big when the performance space was so small, but when she looked around more carefully, she could see the answer for herself. All the equipment needed to make the TV show was spread around in the black part of the room. There were lots of cameras on large stands, and a couple looked as if they were mounted on cranes. Black cables snaked everywhere and a huge fan stood in one corner. What with microphone booms, folding chairs, and strange equipment that Chloe couldn't identify, the space was very cluttered.

There were lots of people around, too. The producer was getting the camera operators to position their cameras exactly where he wanted them, and technicians were putting the finishing touches to the set and the sound equipment. One was assembing the studio drum set right in front of the sparkly star.

"That's an awesome drum set," said Danny happily. "I can't wait to play it."

"You'll be able to try it soon," said Julie. "The producer will want to double-check the camera positions with some people in place and then they'll need to get the sound levels right for all of you, so you'll have to take your turn. Who's up first?" She consulted her clipboard. "Oh, not your band, Danny. It's the other one. Where are you?" She smiled at the students as they came forward. "The technicians will be here for another ten minutes," she told them. "You can do your sound check right afterward. Then it's Ayesha and Rob, and after that, Zil, it's your band. Then ..."

Chloe's stomach did a flip, and she took a deep

breath. Soon, very soon, she would be standing on that gleaming white floor doing her sound check. And then, a little later, she would be giving the performance of her life.

8. Almost There!

It wasn't long before Chloe and the rest of the band were called for their sound check. Nervously, they made their way to the performance space and Danny slid behind the drum set. Chloe had to wait while the sound engineer listened to Danny play each of his drums in turn. And once the levels were set for the way Danny played the drums, the engineer asked Jeff to play a few bars of his bass. It was Lenny's turn next and then Zil's.

Chloe swallowed. Her throat felt terribly dry. Would she be able to make any sound at all when the engineer wanted to set the level for her voice? It was one thing to sing a few lines at school for Mr. Timms so he could set the levels right for a performance or a recording in the school studio, but this was different. Would this engineer be impatient with her if she messed things up?

But it was all right. To Chloe's relief, he was very friendly and she was well able to sing a couple of lines into her microphone for him.

"That's fine," he told her. "Could you all play together now, please?"

Danny counted them in and they ran through their song.

"That's it," said the engineer. "Your sound levels are good. Do you have any problems?"

"I can't hear myself very well," said Chloe.

Until she had sung with the band, Chloe had sometimes wondered what the black boxes were that all bands seemed to have in front of them when they played. Now she knew. The audience could hear a band because the speakers pointed out toward them, but the band needed to hear what they were doing as well. The black boxes were extra speakers called monitors that played the band's music back to them. In the Rock Department, Chloe's voice was played back to her through a monitor, but the studio had given her a small earpiece to wear instead and the sound wasn't coming through.

"What's the problem?" asked the engineer.

"Zil's guitar is too loud in my ear," said Chloe. "I need less of him and more of me."

The engineer adjusted the sounds going into Chloe's earpiece and they tried again.

"It's still not right," she said, feeling really embarrassed and very worried. But it wasn't her fault that the levels weren't quite right, and it was vital for her to be able to hear well.

The engineer played around with all the levels, but poor Chloe still wasn't getting the right sound. Everybody was beginning to look jittery. Time was ticking by and there were other acts to sound-check before the start of the program.

"How is it now?" asked the engineer.

But this time Chloe couldn't hear *anything* in her

earpiece at all. "I'm sorry," she said, close to tears. She was losing her confidence now. Maybe it wasn't a technical problem. Was she doing something stupid? It was awful having such an important thing go wrong just before the program was supposed to start. *What will I do if they can't figure it out?* Chloe asked herself. *If I can't hear, I might come in at the wrong time and ruin the whole song!* It was every singer's worst nightmare and it was happening now, at the Rising Stars Concert.

The engineer's assistant brought Chloe another earpiece. "Maybe the problem is at this end," she told her kindly. "Let's try this one."

Sure enough, it was the earpiece that had caused all the problems. Chloe gave a great sigh of relief.

"These things happen," said the assistant, smiling encouragingly at Chloe. "Don't let it throw you off."

Chloe knew the assistant was right. She shouldn't allow a technical hitch to unsettle her just before she was scheduled to perform.

"How are the levels for you now?" asked the engineer.

Chloe gave him the thumbs-up. "It's *much* better, thank you," she told him. "Now I can hear what I'm doing and what everyone else is playing, too."

They ran through the song again and this time it went really well. But there were still the cameras to consider.

"Make the camera your friend," the producer advised them. "Yes, you have a small live audience, but don't neglect the camera. That is your audience, too."

Chloe was thrilled at this piece of advice. She'd read about making the camera her friend a long time ago, before she'd even gotten to Rockley Park School. She'd practiced in her bedroom long before she'd had any idea that she would be able to do it for real. Now she could put all her practice to the test!

When the sound checks were finished, the students went back to their rehearsal room to wait for their call. It was difficult, all this waiting. While they were doing something, Chloe's nervousness disappeared, but as soon as she sat down in the rehearsal room, her anxiety came flooding back. So she found a quiet corner and did some breathing exercises that Mr. Player had taught her. They did calm her down, but Chloe was sure the only thing that would really help would be to get back onto that small white circle and perform. She joined the others again. There really wasn't long to go now.

"I wonder what everyone is doing back at school?" she said to Danny, who was trying to twirl his drumsticks and not doing it very well, although he was usually very good at it.

He looked at his watch. "It's almost time for dinner," he said. "They'll be coming out of French." He twirled his sticks again and dropped them both.

"I don't think you should try that on TV," said Zil.

"Don't worry," said Danny. "I won't!"

Just then, Chloe's cell phone vibrated and she pulled it out of her pocket.

"Mine's going off too!" said Danny.

Chloe looked at her text. *Thinking of you. Break a leg. Love Lolly, Pop, and Tara.*

"I got one from them as well," said Danny, when Chloe showed him the text. "Oh, and Marmalade's sent one, too. He never usually texts people." He showed her his cell phone. "Look, it's for you as well."

Chloe read the text. *Friends, make me proud!* it said. Chloe giggled. Trust Marmalade not to put anything obvious like "good luck." But it was nice to know that people were thinking about them. Everyone at school knew what time the performance was going to take place, so they must have realized that dinnertime was a good opportunity to send their best wishes.

Very soon now the audience would be arriving and settling into their seats. No one knew exactly who would show up, but there would certainly be some important people there. That knowledge only added to Chloe's last-minute nerves.

Would she remember all that she'd learned? When the program was eventually shown on TV, she knew all her friends from Rockley Park and beyond would be watching. Her family would watch it, too. She simply couldn't let all those people down. And what about Mr. Player? He had spent hours helping her to get the best out of her voice. Now Chloe wanted to show him that she had taken to heart all that he had said. She wanted to do it for him and for Judge Jim, who had always encouraged her. She wanted to do it for her friends and family, too, but most of all, Chloe wanted to make a success of this concert for herself and the rest of the band.

As Chloe was thinking this, everyone else was quiet, too, mentally readying themselves for the performance of their lives. Then the door opened and Julie came in.

"It's time," she said.

9. Chloe Sings

The first act followed Julie out of the room, and the remaining students cheered them on.

"Go for it!"

"Break a leg."

"You can do it!"

The door closed behind them and the room fell silent. The other band had looked very nervous. Chloe hoped they'd be all right. Just then, a screen mounted high on the wall flickered into life, and the students could see the studio for themselves. The audience was there and waiting for the first act to appear.

"Fantastic!" said Zil. "I didn't realize we'd be able to see the concert, too."

The band got into position and their drummer counted them in. Chloe watched carefully. Shots from all the cameras were being fed to the monitor and sometimes she could see clips of the audience reaction.

"Mrs. Sharkey is there!" said Jeff, pointing at the screen.

"Where?" asked Chloe.

"I just caught a glimpse of her as the camera panned over the audience."

Then they saw her again. Mr. Player laughed at the students' excitement. "You didn't think the principal would miss this, did you? It's the high point of the school year for her."

"I guess so," said Lenny. "It just hadn't occurred to me she'd be there. I feel much better now that I know she's backing us up."

Chloe felt the same. Mrs. Sharkey could be pretty scary, but somehow it *was* reassuring to see her in the audience.

In no time, the first band had finished their

performance. They arrived back in the room looking relieved that it was over. Ayesha and Rob were already on their feet.

"Break a leg!" Chloe called out as the two singers disappeared with Julie.

Danny picked up his drumsticks and put them down again. He beat out a nervous rhythm with his fingers on his leg. It was almost their turn.

Ayesha and Rob were fantastic. They sang wonderfully together, and Chloe was sure the TV audience would love them. Their performance was impressive and truly professional.

But now Julie was back, waiting to take Chloe and the boys along to the studio. Chloe jumped up. Suddenly she didn't feel ready, even after all the time they'd spent waiting for this moment. But she had wanted to be a Rising Star ever since she had started at Rockley Park. She *had* to be ready. She took a deep breath.

I can do this, she told herself. *Of course I can. I'll be fine.* It felt so right being here. This was what she was made for. Yes. Of course she could do it. As long as no one made a mistake.

"Make sure you leave your cell phones behind," warned Julie.

Chloe put her phone on the table, the makeup lady flicked a last spot of powder on her cheeks, and they were ready to go.

Chloe exchanged a nervous smile with Danny. This was it. It was their turn now. She and the boys bunched together behind Julie.

"Ready?" she asked. They all nodded nervously. In a moment, they were in the narrow hallway heading toward the brightly lit studio. Rob and Ayesha were coming toward them, and Chloe could see that Ayesha's eyes were bright with excitement.

"Give it all you've got," she said to Chloe as they met. But there was no time for a reply. Chloe had to hurry to keep up with the boys. Then they were at the studio door and Julie opened it for them. All the lights were on and the space was ready.

It was strange walking back onto the white circle

with rows of people watching. Chloe had never before had a real audience so close to where she was performing, before. As she and the band appeared, the audience applauded but the clapping sounded very thin because there were so few people there. It felt very hot under the powerful lights, and Chloe had to work hard not to lose her concentration.

She had been told to watch for the small light on each camera that showed when it was filming. *Think of the camera as your friend*, she told herself firmly, and smiled into camera two as if she didn't have a care in the world. Danny slid behind the drum set and the rest of the boys picked up their guitars. Chloe took her microphone from its stand, Zil played the opening chord, and they were off!

For the first couple of bars they were feeling their way and Chloe was afraid that the song wouldn't sound confident enough. Then she reminded herself to listen to Danny. He was playing away as reliably as ever. All they had to do was listen to his beat and keep to the same rhythm. If they did that, they couldn't go wrong. She turned toward the band to give them some encouragement and just then Zil caught her eye and grinned. Chloe felt herself grinning back and hoped that the cameras had caught the moment.

But now they were reaching the critical part of the song. Lenny's riff was coming up and Chloe's heart started thumping.

Keep calm, she told herself. She couldn't allow herself to panic or her breathing would be affected and then she wouldn't be able to sing properly. *Come on, Lenny. You can do it,* she thought. *Don't make me have to help you out!*

She turned to glance at him and to her horror she could see that he was beginning to panic, too. She had to sing one more line and then his riff would take over, but poor Lenny looked as if he'd already decided that he would probably flub it. She gave him an encouraging look and delivered her line perfectly for him, willing him to succeed.

His first few notes were fine, but then he got to the part he often stumbled over and began to mess it up.

Chloe couldn't leave him hanging. She had to do something to help. If he had a few seconds to compose himself, maybe he would be able to manage it if they could give him a chance to try again?

There were no words to go with the riff, so Chloe opened her mouth and sang the notes once for him in her clear voice. She looked at Zil, who nodded slightly and played up to the riff again. Chloe repeated the line for Lenny. He was still struggling, so she sang the riff once more. This time, when it came around again, Lenny was ready. He nodded at her gratefully and took over.

He was so nearly note-perfect that Chloe felt like cheering. Instead she allowed herself another glance in Lenny's direction. Their eyes met and Lenny smiled. But it was important that Chloe didn't miss her cue to sing the next verse and Zil was watching her anxiously. She beamed him a smile and he looked reassured.

Chloe's confidence was soaring now. The band was rocking, and her voice was doing the song justice, but she wanted to give it something extra. She had belted out the first verse and sang the chorus with Zil backing her, but when she went into the second verse her mind was racing ahead to a line she had always liked. As she approached it, she brought her voice down and glanced at Danny. His drumming followed her mood and grew gentler. She could sense Zil's surprise, but he followed and so did the other two. Instead of singing the line, Chloe almost said it, quietly but with great feeling.

She glanced back at Danny again and nodded. He picked up the beat once more and the guitarists followed.

She sang the rest of the verse in the best rock tradition. The band was really going for it now. Danny was thrashing his drums and Zil's lead was a triumph. They finished with perfect timing, as if they were one person instead of five.

They bowed and waved into the cameras as the audience applauded. Chloe felt terrific. It had gone better than she could have possibly dreamed! They had all had the chance to demonstrate their own particular skills individually, and together the band members had sounded fantastic.

As soon as they got back to the rehearsal room, they were greeted with whoops of approval from the other students. Chloe had just enough time to give her encouragement to the next act, and then she was engulfed in waves of enthusiasm from the remaining students and the teachers.

"That was *so* good!" Judge Jim told the band. "You were all fantastic."

"What gave you the idea to speak that line instead of singing it?" asked Zil.

"I don't know," said Chloe, a little embarrassed now that it was over. "I'm sorry. It just suddenly came to me. Was it all right?"

"You shouldn't introduce new ideas when it's such an important performance," said Jeff. "We might have messed up!"

"But we didn't," said Danny. "I could tell what you wanted, Chloe. You communicated really well. And that line was inspired."

"And thanks for helping me out," said Lenny. "I really panicked there for a minute."

"You covered for him so well," said Zil. "I'm sure everyone will think we were supposed to do it like that."

"You played your riff perfectly in the end," Chloe said to Lenny. "I wanted to cheer!"

"I'm glad you didn't." Danny laughed.

"Thank you for letting me sing with you," Chloe said seriously. "I never thought I would say this, but I loved it."

"Did you love it enough to do it again sometime?" asked Mr. Player.

Chloe looked at him. "Yes," she told him. "It's very different from what I'm used to, but it was super exciting performing with a real band. I wouldn't have traded it for anything!"

"Well, let's hope something comes of it," said Zil.

"Don' worry," said Judge Jim. "There are plenty of important people out there, and you'll get a chance to talk to them in the hospitality room afterward."

"We will?" said Chloe, feeling panicky again. "I won't know what to say."

"It's just a party," said Judge Jim. "All you have to do is enjoy yourself."

"Okay," said Chloe. "I think I can manage that."

10. Party Time

Julie escorted the last performer back from the studio, and this time, instead of leaving right away, she came in and sat down. She waited while the students congratulated Isla.

"Good job, Isla! You were fantastic," one of the other senior students told her.

Chloe had to admit that Isla had made the most of her opportunity and had ended the concert on a real high. Her cool, bluesy voice had really wowed the audience. She would be leaving school soon and fully deserved to make it big. A Rockley Park education had turned Isla into an accomplished and mature singer, and Chloe fervently hoped the school would do the same for her.

Once everyone had calmed down, Julie stood up to get their attention. "Well," she began. "Congratulations from me, too. You've all been wonderful performers and so easy to take care of. Thank you for being so professional."

A warm glow crept through Chloe's body. It was so nice to be praised like that by someone who had probably seen countless stars.

"If you're ready, I'll take you through to the hospitality suite, where you can mingle with the audience and have a snack before you go back to school. Okay? Follow me."

Danny walked with Chloe. "I'm starving," he said. "I hope they're big snacks."

Chloe laughed. "Didn't you eat any of the pizza they gave us for lunch?"

"Not much," Danny replied. "But I'm definitely hungry now."

"Me, too," agreed Chloe, realizing suddenly how ravenous she was.

The hospitality suite wasn't as impressive as it had sounded. It was just another room, filled with members of the audience who were all talking loudly together. However, when they saw the students coming in, they began to applaud. Chloe felt very overwhelmed.

For a few minutes, the students stayed bunched together, not sure what to do. Then a waiter came up to them with a tray of food.

"I wonder who the most important person in the room is?" said Chloe, nibbling chips and looking around at everyone. Most of them looked very ordinary. But it was impossible to tell.

"How about him?" said Danny, pointing out a man with a very bright tie and a leather jacket. "Maybe he's the head of a big record company."

"Sorry to disappoint you," said Mr. Player, who was standing nearby. "I happen to know he's a reporter with the local paper. In fact, I'd better go and have a word with him. Excuse me."

With that, he was gone. Danny looked at Chloe and shrugged.

"Well, I figure the A&R people will come up to us if they're interested," said Chloe.

"I hope so," said Danny.

Someone *was* coming over to the two friends, but it was a person they already knew.

"How's it goin'?" said Judge Jim. "Got enough to eat?"

"Yes, thanks," said Chloe.

"There's someone over here who'd like to speak to you," Judge Jim continued to Danny. "Let me introduce you." Without further ado, he took Danny away with him, and Chloe was left on her own.

For a few minutes, she didn't mind too much. It was fun watching everyone talking. Judge Jim had taken Danny over to a large man wearing a flamboyant hat. The man was grinning at Danny and now he had handed him what looked like a business card. A pang of jealousy ran through Chloe. It looked like Danny had someone interested in him, but it seemed no one wanted to speak to her. Hadn't her performance impressed *anyone*?

She wondered about going over to Zil, but he was talking seriously to the rest of the boys in the band, and Chloe didn't want another postmortem of their performance. There wasn't anyone she wanted to speak to because she didn't know who any of these adults were. Anyway, even if she had recognized any record-company scouts, what would she say to them? Everyone here had seen her perform. If they thought she was worth a recording contract, they would seek her out.

"Hello, Chloe. You did very well today. Well done." It was the school principal, Mrs. Sharkey.

"Thank you," she replied politely. But before Mrs. Sharkey could say any more, an elderly woman was introducing herself and Mrs. Sharkey was drawn away. Chloe wandered over to a table of food and drinks and found some tasty dips. But after all the excitement of the performance, she was feeling a little deflated now.

Soon the crowd thinned out as people began to leave. Judge Jim started rounding up the students, and once they were all together, they made their way out of the studio building and back to the minibus.

Everyone got on the bus and Judge Jim counted them.

"Where's Mr. Player?" he asked.

"Someone grabbed him just as he was about to come out," Danny said. "But he told me to tell you that he wouldn't be long."

"Okay. No worries," said Judge Jim. "We can wait." He slipped a CD into the minibus's player.

"That guy with the big hat, he's an agent," said Danny excitedly. "He really liked what I did. He said he might be in touch. Look. He gave me his card."

"Wow," said Chloe, trying not to sound envious. She took the card and looked at it. It was very glossy and impressive-looking. No wonder Danny was excited.

She looked out of the window and told herself not to be silly. There was plenty of time for agents and record companies to become interested in her. This was only her first year at Rockley Park. She had *years* to go before she needed to think seriously about a career.

And didn't all the teachers say that slow and steady was the best way of approaching a career in the music business? So many people who had become stars overnight or at a young age very soon faded into obscurity. Others found it impossible to handle fame that came so quickly.

Chloe wanted to be in the business for a long time. She didn't want instant stardom followed by nothing. Even so, it was hard to stay positive when other students were getting all the attention. After all, Danny was her age and *he* was drawing interest.

"Hurray!" A cheer went up as Mr. Player appeared and climbed into the minibus. Judge Jim started the engine, but Mr. Player didn't sit down.

"Where's Chloe?" he asked, scanning the seats.

"Here," said Chloe, wondering what was wrong.

"You're looking a little down in the mouth, Chloe," Mr. Player said. "Didn't you enjoy the party?"

"It was all right," said Chloe.

"Well, cheer up. You did really well today. You should be proud of yourself. Oh, and I got you this." Mr. Player handed her a small white card. It was printed with a name and address Chloe didn't recognize.

"What is it?" she asked.

Mr. Player grinned and ruffled Chloe's hair. "It's a business card," he told her.

"Yes, but..." The cards Danny and Zil had been given had a company logo and contact details on them, but this was just a plain white card with someone's name and address on it.

Danny peered over her shoulder. "Is it from a recording company?" he asked doubtfully.

"I don't think so," said Chloe, remembering the impressive card he'd been given.

"No, it's not from a recording company," said Mr. Player with a very pleased expression on his face. "It's better than that!"

Chloe and Danny exchanged glances. What could be better than interest from a recording company?

"The card came from Manny Williams's assistant," Mr. Player told her. "Have you heard of Manny Williams?"

Chloe nodded. Every singer at Rockley Park had

heard of *him*. He was a highly respected independent producer who was very choosy about the people he worked with.

"Well, Manny's assistant thought Manny might be interested in hearing you sing solo," Mr. Player told Chloe. "That was who held me up just now," he added, turning to Judge Jim. "She was asking if we could set up a meeting next semester so Manny could hear Chloe." He turned back. "Is that all right?" he asked.

Chloe's head was whirling. Manny Williams? Might be interested in *her*? He chose so few artists to work with. Okay, this was only his assistant's opinion, but she must have a good idea of the type of talent he was looking for. If Manny Williams decided to work with her, the whole music industry would take notice. He was famous for picking people who ended up being seriously big stars!

"Is that all right?" Mr. Player repeated.

Chloe looked up at him, her eyes shining. She couldn't speak. After thinking no one was interested in her, this sudden news was such a shock. Chloe swallowed. Still speechless, she nodded several times. As she did so, she could hear Judge Jim's big, warm laugh rolling around the bus as he put it into gear.

Zil gave her an encouraging smile, and Danny's grin made it obvious that he was sharing Chloe's feelings.

She sank back in her seat, still gripping the plain little card tightly in her hand. What a roller coaster of a year this had been! Behind her was an awful lot of hard work. Ahead, there would probably be lots of ups and downs as she tried to make her way as a singer. But for *now*, Chloe really *was* a Rising Star!

✳ **So you want**
to be a pop star?
✳

Turn the page to read some top tips
on how to make your dreams
✳ *come true....* ✳

✳ *Making it in the music biz* ✳

Think you've got tons of talent?
Well, music maestro Judge Jim Henson,
Head of Rock at talent academy Rockley Park,
has put together his top tips to help
you become a superstar....

 Number One Rule: Be positive!
You've got to believe in yourself.

✳ Be active! Join your school choir
or form your own band.

✳ Be different! Don't be afraid to stand
out from the crowd.

✳ Be determined! Work hard and stay focused.

✳ Be creative! Try writing your own material—
it will say something unique about you.

✳ Be patient! Don't give up if things
don't happen overnight.

 Be ready to seize opportunities
when they come along.

Be versatile! Don't have a one-track mind—try out new things and gain as many skills as you can.

 Be passionate! Don't be afraid to show some emotion in your performance.

 Be sure to watch, listen, and learn all the time.

Be willing to help others. You'll learn more that way.

 Be smart! Don't neglect your schoolwork.

Be cool and don't get bigheaded! Everyone needs friends, so don't leave them behind.

Always stay true to yourself.

And finally, and most important, enjoy what you do!

Go for it! It's all up to you now....

CINDY JEFFERIES's varied career has included being a Venetian-mask maker and a video DJ. Cindy decided to write *Fame School* after experiencing the ups and downs of her children, who have all been involved in the music business. Her insight into the lives of wannabe pop stars and her own musical background mean that Cindy knows how exciting and demanding the quest for fame and fortune can be.

Cindy lives on a farm in Gloucestershire, England, where the animal noises, roaring tractors, and rehearsals of Stitch, her son's indie-rock band, all help her write!

To find out more about Cindy Jefferies, visit her Web site: www.cindyjefferies.co.uk